SACRAMENTO PUBLIC LIBRARY
D1133076

WONDER BOOKS®

Oceans

A Level Two Reader

By Cynthia Klingel and Robert B. Noyed

Plants and animals live in many different places. One of these places is the ocean.

Many plants, fish, and other animals live in the ocean. Most of them live near the surface of the water. There, sunlight makes the water warmer.

The ocean can be very deep. The deep water is dark and cold. No sunlight reaches this water.

Many animals have learned how to live in the ocean. There are hundreds of different kinds of fish.

Some fish are as small as a pin. Some are bigger than a car! Fish come in many different colors.

Some fish can be scary.
Sharks and other fish have
sharp teeth.

Many fish live in coral reefs. Coral reefs are made up of the skeletons of tiny sea animals. The reefs are colorful and very beautiful.

Other animals live in the ocean, too. They include crabs, eels, whales, dolphins, and turtles. Many animals in the ocean eat ocean plants.

Many ocean animals eat plants that grow underwater. Some of these plants look like tall grass. Others have bright colors.

The ocean is beautiful and interesting. It is home to plants and animals that live nowhere else. It is a special place.

Index

animals, 3, 4, 8, 15, 16, 19, 20
coral reef, 15
crabs, 16
deep water, 7
dolphins, 16
eels, 16
fish, 4, 8, 11, 12, 15
plants, 3, 4, 16, 19, 20
sharks, 12
sunlight, 4, 7
surface, 4
turtles, 16
whales, 16

To Find Out More

Books

Frasier, Debra. *Out of the Ocean.* New York: Harcourt Brace, 1998.

Rothaus, Don P. *Oceans.* Chanhassen, Minn.: The Child's World, 1997.

Simon, Seymour. *Oceans.* New York: William Morrow, 1997.

Web Sites

Aquatic Safari
http://www.seaworld.org/VirtualAquarium/aquaticsafari.html
To learn about all sorts of creatures living in the ocean.

The Evergreen Project: Marine Ecosystems
http://mbgnet.mobot.org/salt/index.html
To find details about all kinds of ocean life.

Note to Parents and Educators

Welcome to The Wonders of Reading™! These books provide text at three different levels for beginning readers to practice and strengthen their reading skills. In addition, the use of nonfiction text gives readers the valuable opportunity to *read to learn*, not just to learn to read.

These leveled readers allow children to choose books at their level of reading confidence and performance. Level One books offer beginning readers simple language, word choice, and sentence structure as well as a word list. Level Two books feature slightly more difficult vocabulary, longer sentences, and longer total text. In the back of each Level Two book are an index and a list of books and Web sites for finding out more information. Level Three books continue to extend word choice and length of text. In the back of each Level Three book are a glossary, an index, and a list of books and Web sites for further research.

State and national standards in reading and language arts emphasize using nonfiction at all levels of reading development. The Wonders of Reading™ books fill the historical void in nonfiction for primary grade readers with the additional benefit of a leveled text.

About the Authors

Cynthia Klingel has worked as a high school English teacher and an elementary teacher. She is currently the curriculum director for a Minnesota school district. Writing children's books is another way for her to continue her passion for sharing the written word with children. Cynthia is a frequent visitor to the children's section of bookstores and enjoys spending time with her many friends, family, and two daughters.

Robert Noyed started his career as a newspaper reporter. Since then, he has worked in communications and public relations for more than fourteen years for a Minnesota school district. He enjoys writing books for children and finds that it brings a different feeling of challenge and accomplishment from other writing projects. He is an avid reader who also enjoys music, theater, traveling, and spending time with his wife, son, and daughter.

Published by The Child's World®, Inc.
PO Box 326
Chanhassen, MN 55317-0326
800-599-READ
www.childsworld.com

Photo Credits
© 2002 A. Witte/C. Mahaney/Stone: 5
© 2000 Bill Curtsinger/Dembinsky Photo Assoc. Inc.: 6
© Frank Siteman/PhotoEdit: 10
© 2002 Jeff Rotman/Stone: 14
© 1999 Marilyn Kazmers/Dembinsky Photo Assoc. Inc.: cover, 17
© 2002 Norbert Wu/Stone: 13
© 2002 Pete Atkinson/Stone: 21
© Randy Morse/Tom Stack & Associates: 18
© 1997 Susan Blanchet/Dembinsky Photo Assoc. Inc.: 2
© Tom & Therisa Stack/Tom Stack & Associates: 9

Project Coordination: Editorial Directions, Inc.
Photo Research: Alice K. Flanagan

Library of Congress Cataloging-in-Publication Data
Klingel, Cynthia Fitterer.
Oceans / by Cynthia Klingel and Robert B. Noyed.
p. cm.
ISBN 1-56766-974-3 (lib. bdg.)
1. Marine biology—Juvenile literature.
2. Ocean—Juvenile literature. [1. Marine biology. 2. Ocean.] I. Noyed, Robert B. II. Title.
QH91.16 .K55 2001
578.77—dc21
00-013180